BEEGU

Alexis Deacon

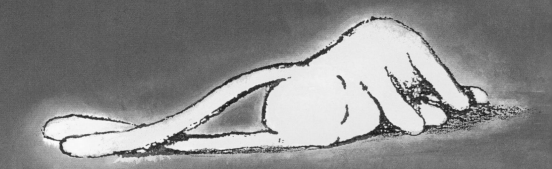

Farrar, Straus and Giroux
New York

for the other

BEEGU

First published in Great Britain by Hutchinson,
an imprint of Random House Children's Books, 2003
Printed and bound in Singapore
First American edition, 2003
1 3 5 7 9 10 8 6 4 2

Library of Congress Cataloging-in-Publication Data

Deacon, Alexis.
    Beegu / Alexis Deacon.— 1st American ed.
       p.   cm.
    Summary: A small creature from space finds no welcome on Earth, until she meets a
group of children on a playground.
    ISBN 0-374-30667-2
    [1. Extraterrestrial beings—Fiction.]   I. Title.

PZ7.D33923Be 2003
[E]—dc21
                                                                    2002192738

Beegu was not supposed to
be here.

She was lost.

No one seemed to understand her.

Some wouldn't even stay still to listen.

From far away

she thought she heard

her mother

calling . . .

Beegu didn't like being alone.

She needed to find some friends.

And she did at last.

But Beegu wasn't
wanted there,
it seemed.

Then she thought she'd found
the perfect place . . .

. . . and it was!

But not everyone thought so . . .

"Wait!"

Her friends
wanted to say goodbye.

Goodbye!

Once again, from far away she thought
she heard her mother calling.
But she knew it couldn't be . . .

. . . could it?

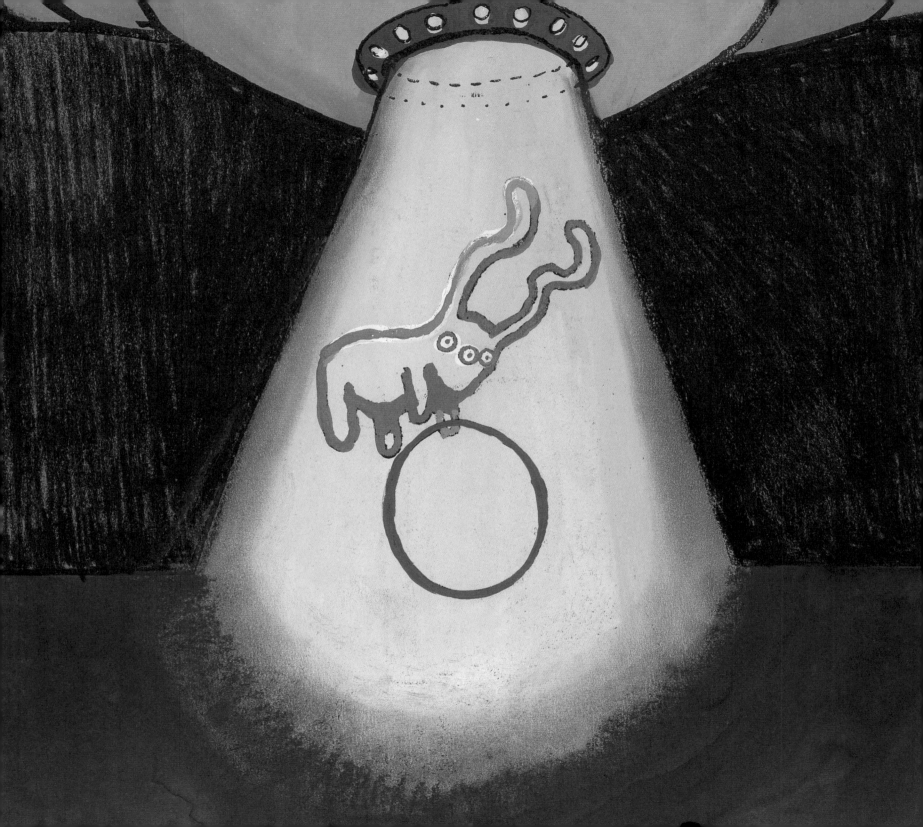

It was!

Beegu told her parents all about life on Earth.
How Earth creatures were mostly big
and unfriendly, but there were some
small ones who seemed hopeful.

Beegu would always remember
those small ones.

She hoped they would remember her too.